THE PRICE OF BRAVERY

ARTA

Serial Number: P2546250259
Title: The Price of Bravery
Authors: Arta Shiri
Layout: Merry Oskooei
ISBN:0-235-77892-1-978
Subject: Short Story, Young Adult
Book format/Size: Paperback, A5
Pages: 18
Publication Date: July 2025
Publisher: Kidsocado Publishing House

Kidsocado Publishing House
Vancouver, Canada

Phone: +1 (236) 333-7248

WhatsApp: +1 (236) 333-7248

Email: info@kidsocado.com

Website: https://kidsocado.com

Address: 2100-1055 West Georgia St,

Vancouver, BC V6E 3P3, Canada

*I would like to dedicate
this book to
my Mom and Dad,
who encouraged me
to publish this book,
and to the soldiers who
fought in WW2,
showing true bravery
in the most difficult of
times.*

Over two months ago, John, Robert, and a few other guys from their school enlisted in the army. They'd grown up together in a small town just outside of Toronto. Growing up, John had never been very athletic; he had an average build, short brown hair, long legs, and blue eyes. He spent most of his time in books and news articles. However, Robert had a large muscular body and black hair—slicked back with so much natural oil it would practically gleam. By eighth grade, he had a neck so large he looked like a tank. Even though they didn't have a team at the time, he'd often play rugby in the small field behind the school, and the other players would show up most weekdays after school.

During the summer, they'd create a few teams, organize tournament-style fixtures, and play games against each other.

The two, John and Robert, lived across the street from each other and naturally grew closer over time, hanging out frequently, and occasionally John would join Robert to play rugby. However, playing rugby and hanging out happened only before the world was at war.

Today would be the end of their second month at boot camp. They were to spend another month training and preparing for things worse than the human mind can fathom.

At the crack of dawn, an instructor burst into the barrack, "FIX!" He bellowed, and they all swiftly fell into line. A stern, stony look on his face, "Fall in for PT!" Neither of the two struggled with the morning jogs, but the obstacle courses posed a challenge for John. Most trainees easily cleared the log hurdles and scaled the plank wall in seconds, but some, including John, struggled greatly with the vertical rope climb, towering 40 ft. in the air. He'd already failed it twice; if it happened once more, he would be unfit to serve.

He spent his free hours training, pushing himself until his forearms were red-hot and felt like they were torn to shreds, getting closer and closer to the top as time passed.

Finally, the day came; he jogged up to the rope out of breath, sweating bullets; he grasped the rope firmly, placing one foot over the other with the rope in between. Gradually, John made his way up, focusing only on the top of the rope. Almost at the top, an instructor yelled at him from below to pick up the pace; he missed his footing and slipped down a bit, burning his hands. He regained stability and started climbing again, 5ft, 3ft, 1ft, he'd made it, he'd passed!

A week later, they were on a boat to France.

They both stood in fear on a line along the muddy trench, waiting for the signal to charge forward. They waited and waited for what felt like an eternity. Suddenly, the whistles blew, and an officer shouted at them both to move up and out. Shells came down in a deafening roar, causing puffs of smoke and kicking dirt into those near; bullets whizzed by, and the screams of wounded soldiers tore through the air.

Amidst the chaos, the two were separated. Suddenly, an explosion erupted, knocking Robert to the floor; he lay there for a minute, unsure what to do. After the realization that he'd lost John sunk in, he scrambled to his feet, yelling, "John! John!" However, his bellow was pointless; his voice was drowned by the never-ending barrage of gunfire and the tearing of the earth around him. The reality of his situation began to sink in: he had to keep moving or die. He moved from cover to cover, stumbling and tripping over the bodies of his fallen brothers, uncertain if he would ever see his friend again.

On the other side of the battlefield, John pressed forward, scanning the terrain for his buddy. A machine gun opened fire; he dove for cover in a crater made by an earlier bombing. He pressed himself into the ground, feeling the pounding of his heart throughout his body and the screams of the wounded drilling into his head.

Readying himself, he waited for a break

in the gunfire to move cover; he stood and then pressed forward, but not quick enough.

A spray of bullets aimed directly at him tore through his torso; he tumbled to the ground, filled with fear as he tried to process the tragedy that had just befell him.

Soon, a sense of calm engulfed him; he knew it would all be over soon. Although it was still daylight, as he lay there staring at the smoky sky, it became darker by the minute, and shortly after, John fell into an abysmal of darkness, never to return again.

After taking a second to regain his bearings, he walked forward, attempting to maintain his balance. The terrain was littered with barbed wire and deep puddles of mud from older craters. He saw a group of guys maybe 10ft ahead of him taking cover behind a broken stone wall, one being dragged onto a stretcher. He sprinted towards them, dodging enemy fire. Crouched by the wall, a barrage of gunfire overhead, he suddenly felt a warm feeling in his thigh. Robert looked down and saw a stream of blood pouring out of his leg; he'd been hit.

Gasping for air and unable to call for help, he stared up, trying to find a gap in the smoke for one final glimpse at the sky. The relentless storm of bullets, the pounding of artillery, and distant screams of agony were all that could be heard as his vision faded and his body was consumed by the earth.

"Stretcher!" He called, and one of the stretcher-bearers rushed over to evaluate the situation. He gave him a shot of morphine and told him to keep pressure on the wound while they took the other guy back to the trenches. He waited, watching as others moved past him, lifeless bodies scattered across the bloody battlefield and more piling up every passing moment. As exhaustion drifted over him, he closed his eyes to rest. The bearer grabbed his shoulders, shaking him awake, "Stay with me, Bud! We're gonna get you out of here!" He yelled. Once behind the trench lines, Robert was swiftly transported by ambulance to the nearest field hospital.

He spent the week filled with worry for

his comrade›s safety but determined to reunite. Every day he'd ask around for his whereabouts, but to no avail. Today, multiple trucks showed up loaded with the corpses of hundreds of men. Chances are his body was on those trucks, he thought. He›d heard word of the casualties they'd suffered over the week, so many that it was easy to forget those were human lives, who were all there to do the same thing as him, except their luck ran out. "Private Jones!" Robert turned, and his commander walked towards him holding a large envelope, "You're going home, son, honourable discharge," he explained. It was all finally over.

The war lasted another two years after his discharge, and Robert seemed to have quickly readjusted to his old life. However, even years later, he couldn't stop thinking about all those who had given up their lives—more precisely, he couldn›t stop thinking about his friend, John. They were too young to experience the ill of war, feel what they felt, and do what they did. He thought of all the mothers and fathers who lost their babies and how he hadn't seen John's parents since his discharge from the army.

Robert packed a light bag and traveled to reunite old memories.

He knocked on the door, and a middle-aged woman opened the door, "Hello, Mrs. Daniels," he said, and immediately she hugged him; he had practically been like a second son to them.

"My condolences," he muttered; Mrs. Daniels couldn't say anything other than to tilt her gaze downward and sigh.

"Come with me, would you?" She said, grabbing keys from a small table by the front door. He followed her to a car and got in. As she drove, she asked Robert how he'd been doing. He explained he had been readjusting well. After about 30 minutes of driving, she pulled over, and the car screeched to a halt. He looked out the window, and they were at a cemetery.

"He'd have liked you to be there, you know," she said, looking at him, "At his burial."

They got out of the car, and he followed

her to a grave marked:

Pvt. John S. Daniels

1897-1916.

He dropped to his knees, unable to control the flow of tears. He'd finally found his friend but in a peaceful perpetual state.

The End

Arta is a young writer based in
Vancouver, Canada.

www.ingramcontent.com/pod-product-compliance
Lightning Source LLC
Chambersburg PA
CBHW070513170726
48291CB00008B/2732